TWISTED JOURNEYS™

JOURNEYS #4

THE TREASURE OF

MOUNT FATE

JEFF LIMKE

ILLUSTRATED BY CLINT HILINSKI

GRAPHIC UNIVERSE · MINNEAPOLIS

Story by Jeff Limke

Pencils and inks by Clint Hilinski

Coloring by Hi-Fi Design

Lettering by Marshall Dillon and Terri Delgado

Copyright © 2007 by Lerner Publishing Group, Inc.

Graphic Universe™ and Twisted Journeys™ are trademarks
of Lerner Publishing Group, Inc.

Graphic Universe
A division of Lerner Publishing Group, Inc.
241 First Avenue North
Minneapolis, MN 55401 U.S.A.

Website address: www.lernerbooks.com

Library of Congress Cataloging-in-Publication Data

Limke, Jeff.
    The treasure of Mount Fate / by Jeff Limke ; illustrations by Clint Hilinski.
        p.   cm.—(Twisted journeys)
    ISBN: 978-0-8225-6205-4 (lib. bdg. : alk. paper)
    1. Graphic novels. I. Hilinski, Clint. II. Title.
PN6727.L53T74 2007
    741.5'973—dc22   2006101596

Manufactured in the United States of America
1 2 3 4 5 6 – DP – 12 11 10 09 08 07

ARE YOU READY FOR YOUR
Twisted Journeys™?

YOU ARE THE HERO OF THE BOOK YOU'RE ABOUT TO READ. YOUR JOURNEYS WILL BE PACKED WITH ADVENTURES IN A WORLD OF MAGIC AND MONSTERS. AND EVERY STORY STARS **YOU!**

EACH PAGE TELLS WHAT HAPPENS TO **YOU** AS YOU EXPLORE MOUNT FATE, SEARCH FOR TREASURE, AND FACE DANGERS YOU NEVER EXPECTED. **YOUR** WORDS AND THOUGHTS ARE SHOWN IN THE **YELLOW BALLOONS.** AND YOU GET TO DECIDE WHAT HAPPENS NEXT. JUST FOLLOW THE NOTE AT THE BOTTOM OF EACH PAGE UNTIL YOU REACH A *Twisted Journeys*™ PAGE. THEN MAKE THE CHOICE **YOU** LIKE BEST.

BUT BE CAREFUL...THE WRONG CHOICE COULD MAKE YOUR ADVENTURING DAYS VERY SHORT!

Above you loom the crags of Mount Fate. The early autumn sun glints off the snow that lines the peak. You push back the guard on your helm and take in the sight.

You dismount from your horse and slide your sword back into the scabbard on your back. You see your breath whirl up into the air. It's dashed away by a sharp wind that rips down the mountain before you. You slap your hands together and smile.

"This is a good place to become a hero." Your voice is a bit raspy from the dry air.

Your horse neighs. The sound echoes. *Snickety-snack*, you pull your sword and look around. Behind you, you hear the *clippety-clop* of your horse. You turn around just in time to see it run down the mountain the way you came.

You're all alone. Just you and your sword stand before the legendary Mount Fate . . . and whatever scared your horse.

You're huffing and puffing by the time the trail ends. Where's the entrance to the caves? The old man in the tavern didn't lie to you, did he?

You tap your foot on the rocky ground and stare up at the sky. It's here, it has to be here. *I just have to look a bit,* you tell yourself. *Poke around a little.*

You push aside a few branches. Behind them is a small hole. It's too small to walk into standing up, but if you bend over or crawl, it'll be easy. You smile again. The cold air that stings your cheeks doesn't bother you anymore.

But behind you, you hear noises. You whirl around. It's a borkadrac!

GO ON TO THE NEXT PAGE.

TWISTED JOURNEYS™

The fearsome and hungry borkadrac moves toward you, hissing. In the village below the mountain, you heard that no one escapes this beast.

WILL YOU...

...pull your sword to fight off this monster?

TURN TO PAGE 42.

...turn and run toward the cave opening?

TURN TO PAGE 54.

Great, more spiders. The only choice
is which ones to fight.

WILL YOU...

face the little spiders?
TURN TO PAGE 93.

face the big spider?
TURN TO PAGE 109.

You climb up the rock. It will be harder for the borkadrac to hit you up here.

The borkadrac steps from the brush, mouth partially open in a sinister grin. Your eyes lock on it. It hisses, spitting the sound as though air is leaking from inside it.

"You want me?" you yell. "Come and get me!"

It growls and charges forward, leaping upward at the last second.

You swing your sword down, missing. The borkadrac's claw strikes your bad ankle. The pain rips through you, and you stumble.

The sword falls from your hand as you reach out and try to grab the rock to get your balance. You feel yourself slipping backward. Your hands scramble for a handhold, but they don't find one.

The last thing you see is the borkadrac. It looks over the edge of the cliff down at you as you fall away from it, the mountain, and the mountain's treasure.

THE END

The heat of the fireball scratches at your neck, stinging as it increases. Maybe you're just tired, but you swear you can hear Alaric's voice from a lesson long ago.

"Fighting skills won't help much when it comes to magic," he says. "Sometimes escape is just a matter of luck."

Now you hear his deep-throated chuckle. "Of course, anyone who's bothered to put a magic trap in your path probably also made sure you wouldn't get very lucky...."

The polished walls of the hallway magnify the light and heat. You squint as you try to see where you're running. You bang against a wall. It's cool to the touch, and it is incredibly tempting to press yourself against it.

The roaring sound of the fireball behind you brings you back to your senses.

GO ON TO THE NEXT PAGE.

GO ON TO THE NEXT PAGE.

11

Maybe you should lie down. Heat rises, so the floor may be the safest place to be. But the entrance to the other hallway is only a bit farther. It's maybe two steps and a leap.

WILL YOU...

...make a run for the entrance?

TURN TO PAGE 52.

...press yourself flat against the floor?

TURN TO PAGE 70.

"RRRAAAWWWRRR!" you scream as you run in, hoping to scare the dragon.

Behind you, you hear Wizard Uchawi say, "That's not a good idea."

"Silly, silly adventurer. You wish to be a hero, so you attack a dragon by yourself." The words echo off the walls.

You feel the air around you whip about, and you see the dragon spread his wings. They're twice as wide as he is big. You swing at one, but you're too slow and too far away.

You turn to look back at the wizard, but all you can see is a golden, glowing globe of light where he should be. "Wizard?" you yell.

"Too late now," you hear him call back.

"I would agree with the wizard. You should have talked first, then acted." Gartrugh's voice seems to come from all around.

The air goes warm, and you know what's going to happen next.

GO ON TO THE NEXT PAGE.

14

GO ON TO THE NEXT PAGE.

You realize Gartrugh is right. He's much too big for you to have ever defeated with your sword, even though it's magic.

But you've issued your challenge, and not to back it up would not be heroic.

You step forward as you slash your sword before you. The dragon dances backward, but not in fear.

"I gave you a chance not to fight me, but still you choose to," Gartrugh says with a sigh. "I do not like this, but you force me to defend myself."

Now, you charge forward, swinging your sword to and fro, and hear the dragon breathe inward. *Here it comes,* you tell yourself.

And you're right. The flame comes down and the last thing you feel is the singeing heat of Gartrugh's flaming breath.

THE END

"What do you mean, you don't know? What's to know?" Wizard Uchawi's neck starts turning red. The color seems to be moving up toward his face. "Do you know how long I've been stuck here?"

You shake your head. You're afraid to help him and afraid not to help him. What if he's lying about being trapped?

"Hello? Is anyone in there?" Wizard Uchawi taps on your head with a cinnamon candy stick. "Do you need some help making a decision?"

"I'm not sure," you say. You hear the bear roar and the birds screech.

"No one ever knows for sure, but time is running out, and in fact it may be too late."

"What do you mean?"

"I mean, those doors will disappear and you'll be stuck here, too. The spell that keeps me here affects all who enter this room."

You feel your neck turn red, then your face. "WHAT!"

You're about to be trapped! But there's a door just a few strides away.

"Go ahead. You're probably quicker than I am." A tear flows down Wizard Uchawi's cheek. "I'll just sit down and play solitaire a few more times..."

WILL YOU...

...rush to the door before your time runs out?

TURN TO PAGE 94.

...stop to grab Wizard Uchawi?

TURN TO PAGE 103.

You swing your sword. The borkadrac twists away in defense, but instead of pushing forward with the sword, you turn and run. Behind you, the beast howls, realizing it has been fooled.

The ground thumps and you hear the brush cracking and breaking behind you as the beast chases you. Just keep running, pump the arms, you tell yourself. Get some distance between you and this...this thing.

Its hisses sound closer. A branch flies by your right ear, scratching your cheek. You check over your shoulder. The borkadrac is just three paces behind, but it's not getting any closer. It's big, but at least it's not very fast.

Ahead, the road turns left, and the brush gets thicker. You should be able to lose the beast there if you can just get out of sight. Everyone knows borkadracs see better than they smell.

The trail branches here. The left branch is wider, while the right branch is overgrown with plants.

Wait, what's that snapping noise behind you? Oh no, it's the borkadrac!

WILL YOU...

... turn to face the borkadrac once and for all?

TURN TO PAGE 30.

...take the path to the right?

TURN TO PAGE 39.

...take the path to the left?

TURN TO PAGE 74.

It missed you before, and it might miss you again.

Then again, it must have *known* it missed you, or it wouldn't be coming back, right?

You press yourself against the wall and try to make yourself as little as possible.

There's no time to run away now. The roaring is loud. It's making your ears ring again.

That ringing is the last thing you hear, as the fireball is very thorough, leaving nothing behind it—not even ash.

THE END

Keep running, you tell yourself, *just keep running.* The beast is too big to catch up on this trail, you hope. You can hear it lumbering about through the brush. It won't surprise you, that's for sure.

Ahead you spy daylight through the brush. That's good. You must be close to the goats' grazing pasture. That means people—and the borkadrac isn't stupid enough to venture out where people could hunt it.

Just a few more feet. Your lungs feel like they're on fire. Your feet are sore. You step forward and feel your foot catch on a root.

Down you tumble. You flail your hands out to catch yourself.

WHOOMP!

You land in a heap. Your ankle feels like someone hit it with a club. But you've got to get up. GOT TO GET UP!

You push yourself up and half run, half stumble toward the blue sky ahead.

GO ON TO THE NEXT PAGE.

You rush toward the sky—only to realize that the trail ends here. You're at the edge of a cliff. Nothing but a big rock stands between you and a very long fall.

WILL YOU...

...climb the rock to fight the borkadrac?
TURN TO PAGE 9.

...stand your ground?
TURN TO PAGE 41.

You turn and run. Your heart beats like a hammer and your breathing is harsh. The air is hot and smells of sulfur. You pump your arms hard. Your feet pound the ground. This is a race for your life.

And you have to hope Wizard Uchawi won't be mad. Why would he be? You only abandoned him, condemned him to stay in that room alone until someone else comes along. Of course, no one else ever will come along because you're going to find the treasure. And once the treasure is gone, no one will have any reason to come here, ever again.

Well, that's how it would have gone if you hadn't spun that stupid wheel, you snarl at yourself.

Sweat drips down your forehead and into your eyes, where it stings. For a second you can't see anything, but you keep run-ning, hoping you don't run into—

WHAM!

GO ON TO THE NEXT PAGE.

"I hope you're not looking for conversation. I'm not very happy with you." Wizard Uchawi knocks you on the head with his staff. It hurts, and you realize you hadn't seen the staff before. You look around and realize the room seems bigger now, filled with more stuff...

...except for a small section on the far side, where a table and a chair sit forlornly.

"Over there. That's your space."

"I said I was sorry. I was wrong." You can't look at him. You're too ashamed.

"That's a good start. We have some time to get over this 'misunderstanding.'"

"How long do we have?"

"I waited nine hundred years for you." Wizard Uchawi plops onto his chair and purses his lips.

Your jaw drops. "Nine hundred years? I'll be dead."

Wizard Uchawi smirks, then goes back to frowning. "Oh no, we don't age in here. We've got all the time we'll need."

THE END

You hated to say no, but it was the only way to get out of the room in time before the doors disappeared.

The echo of Wizard Uchawi yelling "Noooooooo" still rings in your ears. He seemed like a likable fellow, but he was too old and too slow.

The air here is dryer, a bit warm, too. Ahead you see a sharp turn, like the one where you found your magic sword. You wonder what's beyond this one. Maybe magic armor?

Instead, you see another turn in the passage, but it's not empty. There's a flat wheel stuck in the ground and a shield emblem beside it. Bricks along the wheel's edges follow a pattern: sword, blank brick, sword, blank brick.

The wheel spins when you touch it, then stops. The shield points at a blank brick.

The air suddenly gets warmer, and you hear a roaring sound.

GO ON TO THE NEXT PAGE.

In the middle of the wheel, a shape forms,
throwing off heat and looking like a—

OH NO, IT'S A FIREBALL!

WILL YOU...

...run ahead?
TURN TO PAGE 10.

...run back the way you came?
TURN TO PAGE 25.

You step forward, keeping your weight on the balls of your feet so you can react quickly. You hold the sword in front of you in a two-handed grip to allow you to block an attack from any side.

You hold your breath, listening for any sound. Nothing. Nothing's moving. You exhale and—

An explosion of twigs, leaves, dirt, and growls bursts through the brush on your left. You turn and ready your sword, but you're too late. The borkadrac's foul-smelling mouth is the last thing you see or smell.

THE END

TWISTED JOURNEYS™

Gartrugh's voice sounds like a hissing snake crossed with a bass drum. But what scares you more than the flames is that he spoke to you. Nobody told you dragons could do that.

WILL YOU...

...pull your sword to fight?

TURN TO PAGE 13.

...run away to save yourself?

TURN TO PAGE 36.

...walk in without drawing your sword?

TURN TO PAGE 89.

You grip your shield and sword so tightly, your knuckles turn white. You swing, the air singing with the sound of metal cleaving stone and the thud of weapons hitting your shield. Three, five, eight soldiers fall before you, but more keep coming.

A sharp pain in your leg makes you wince. You look down and see a small cut. But that isn't what hurts...Your leg is changing. It looks like stone.

You keep fighting, but your leg doesn't move easily. Nor does your foot.

Oh no. You realize where these soldiers came from. They were like you once, adventurers looking for treasure. They fought the stone army in this hallway, just as you are fighting now.

You stop fighting and stand still. The soldiers stop, too. Every one of them understands: You are the newest stone soldier to join this little army forever.

THE END

THE END

You rub the lamp three times. It grows warm, then shakes and twists, trying to break free.

"Tell the genie to come out," yells Wizard Uchawi.

"I command you, genie, as your master, to come out!" The room fills with thunder and a whirling wind.

The genie bows. "What would you have me do, master, for your first of three wishes?"

"I wish to have all the treasure packed for travel and for you to send those heroes home safely," you say.

"Very good." The genie claps. The treasure appears, packed in carts pulled by mules, and the heroes vanish. "And what of your next wish?"

You wink at the wizard. "All in good time, genie."

"I agree. You have chosen well, young hero," says the Lady of the Mount, who has appeared suddenly from out of thin air.

You point toward the door. "Time for us to go home rich and famous, Uchawi," you say as the mules begin walking.

THE END

The rooster's crowing wakes you. As you rub your eyes, you think, *What a strange dream*.

Once dressed, you make your way to breakfast. Your mother stands over a pot, stirring. "I had a very odd dream," you tell her.

She smiles. "Tell me about it."

You sit on the wood bench as she ladles porridge into a bowl in front of you. "Well, I was older and wanting to be a hero, so I went to find the treasure of Mount Fate."

Your mother crinkles her eyebrows. "Mount Fate? That's a dangerous place."

"It was only a dream, Mother." You drone on about the wizard and the Lady of the Mount. But in your mind you're thinking: Someday when you're older and Alaric has taught you more, you're going to go there and find that treasure.

Yes, that would be quite the adventure.

THE END

No wonder the sword is so light. It's magic.
Good thing—the stone soldiers are closing in.
Over your shoulder, you spot a door behind
you that you hadn't noticed.

WILL YOU...

...quickly check the door?

TURN TO PAGE 75.

...keep shuffling backward and
ignore the door?

TURN TO PAGE 96.

The borkadrac doesn't follow you. Everything seems peaceful. The mountain birds chirp a little song, and bees are buzzing.

SNAP! Something snags your ankle. You're knocked backward, and your left leg is yanked upward. You smack your head on the ground. Things go a bit blurry.

Seconds later, you're staring down at the ground where you had stood. You realize you're hanging from a tree branch, bobbing by your leg. Someone must have laid a trap on this path. Well, you'll just take your sword and cut—

Wait, your sword isn't in your hand. Where is it?

You tilt your head back, and there it is. On the path below. Out of reach.

Just as you begin to yell for help, you see some bones to the side of the road. Looks like you weren't the first one to make the wrong choice on this trail.

THE END

"Should we go on?" Wizard Uchawi asks with a sly grin. "There could be worse dangers to face." He's right, you realize. Alaric never taught you how to fight against magic fireballs.

WILL YOU...

... go down the corridor?
TURN TO PAGE 60.

... go through the hole?
TURN TO PAGE 106.

You plant your feet wide, grip the sword in two hands, and raise it over your head. Your ankle throbs in pain.

Emerging from the brush, the borkadrac sees you and charges. It swipes at you, claws extended. You swing the sword down. The edge of the blade cuts into the monster's paw.

The borkadrac roars in pain as you pull back the sword, pivoting on your feet. Your ankle protests. Pain shoots up your leg. You stumble but catch yourself.

The beast spots your weakness. Its tail whipsaws from the side. It strikes your calf, pulling your leg out from under you and sending you to the ground. Your sword slips from your grip and clatters just out of reach.

The borkadrac moves forward with slow steps, mouth wide, saliva dripping. Its tongue snakes about.

Now, unfortunately, you'll learn the answer to the question of whether it will eat you in one bite or two.

THE END

You draw your sword and swing, just like your mentor, Alaric the Brave, taught you. Of course, you fought only little kobolds when he trained you, not hungry borkadracs. But this is how Alaric earned his name, and now you will too.

The borkadrac's breath smells rotten, and his skin looks oily. You inhale deeply, hold the breath a moment, and exhale as you swing. The sword whooshes as it cuts through the air. You miss!

The borkadrac strikes. Its teeth snap, snagging a bit of your cloak, but not you. You turn and swing, cutting the beast just above one leg. Your sword snags a bit and throws you off balance. You stumble and catch yourself, but the beast is already moving toward you.

GO ON TO THE NEXT PAGE.

TWISTED JOURNEYS™

You're using every piece of the training you received from Alaric. But you don't know how long it—or you—will last.

WILL YOU...

...turn and run down the path away from the borkadrac?

TURN TO PAGE 71.

...continue this fight?

TURN TO PAGE 18.

The Lady of the Mount touches your head. Everything goes white.

You open your eyes. It's dark, but you can still see. Catching a whiff of the air, you cough.

"My thoughts, too," says Wizard Uchawi, who's standing next to you.

Around you, everything twinkles. Diamonds seem to be scattered about. In fact, it looks as though some are hanging in the air, like stars. That doesn't seem right.

Something wet spatters your arm, dripping slowly. It burns a little. You try to shake it off. It sticks, not much coming loose at all. The bit that does hits the ground with a gross plop.

Wizard Uchawi lights up his wand. What you see is unbelievable. Huge blobs of clear, murky ooze glop about. Inside the ooze you can see coins, gems, rocks, dirt, and— no, that can't be right. But it is. Those are bones. Human bones.

46 GO ON TO THE NEXT PAGE.

The smoky air burns as you breathe it. It's hard to keep your eyes open. When you try, the air burns them, making them water. Your joints feel weak, like you have the flu.

You cough hard. Your lungs burn, and your throat is raw. The fire was a bad idea. The smoke has poisoned the air.

As you blink, tears run down the side of your face. You look at Wizard Uchawi, but he's not moving. You push his shoulder. He still doesn't move. He seems asleep.

You try to stand, but your legs don't work and you feel tired. Just a little nap to get your strength. That's all you need.

You close your eyes, never to wake up again.

THE END

You press the up arrow, and the doors open to reveal a spiral staircase leading up. The steps are moving, so all you have to do is hop on.

"Pretty nifty," says Wizard Uchawi. "I'd heard about these but never expected to see one. Doesn't use magic, you know?"

You're not interested. The stairs move up, and soon you can see the sky above you. You feel a bit dizzy from the turning. At the top, you step off onto a small platform.

The air is cold, and you can see your breath. You're standing on the top of Mount Fate. Wizard Uchawi stands beside you. "Thanks," he says as he begins to glow and float upward. "Make sure to look me up if you're ever in River City," he yells back at you. A bit of his stuff begins to float after him—a rope, boxes, and a birdcage.

It looks like you'll be stuck up here all alone.

GO ON TO THE NEXT PAGE.

TWISTED JOURNEYS™

You run alongside, yelling at Wizard Uchawi to stop, but he keeps moving. But his belongings, including the rope, are quite close to you, floating like he is.

WILL YOU...

...stop and watch everything fly away?
TURN TO PAGE 95.

...reach out and grab at his rope?
TURN TO PAGE 77.

It's wet in here, and with every step you feel like you could slip. Sharp stones stick up from the uneven floor. If you fall, they could cut you quite badly.

Every so often, you see a small indentation where sections have been carved out of the rock. Somebody has been mining here, not carving a way around the cave-in as you had guessed. Maybe there really is treasure here. Goblins have been known to mine for valuable rocks. This tunnel could very well be a goblin mine.

Just as you're ready to take a step, a flash catches your eye...again. Maybe you'll be lucky twice.

You stop, kneel down, and look closely at a shiny spot. It looks like flecks of gold. With the point of your sword, you tap it, dislodging the loose rock around it. YES! IT'S GOLD!

51

You take what feel like two of the longest steps you have ever taken and dive into the hall.

You cover your ears, trying to block out the fireball's roar. Your ears ring. You press your eyes closed. You inhale deeply and hold it.

A flash of heat bathes you and then passes. Still holding your breath, you wait.

Nothing. No noise. You open one eye. Nothing moves. A torch flickers back to life. You exhale and begin to breathe again. The light of the hallway washes over you. The roar of the fireball seems to be growing fainter, but it's hard to tell with the ringing in your ears. You're sure that if someone were next to you screaming, you wouldn't hear a thing.

But you made it. You survived.

No, wait—the roaring is getting louder…again.

GO ON TO THE NEXT PAGE.

It seems impossible—but the fireball is whooshing toward you again! It almost seems to be tracking you.

WILL YOU...

...crawl back deeper into the hallway?
TURN TO PAGE 104.

...stay where you are?
TURN TO PAGE 21.

It's a tight fit, and as you dive into the cave, your cloak snags on a rock. You pull on it. The borkadrac's thumping gets closer. With a final tug, you pull the cloak free. You hear a loud ripping sound, and you're sure that somewhere your Nana must know you've torn the cloak she sewed for you. Of course, you tell yourself, she'll be more than happy that you're alive to be scolded rather than in some borkadrac's belly for lunch.

You tumble down a slight incline of silt and gravel while the borkadrac howls in frustration. It's too big to follow you.

At the bottom of the slope, you pull yourself to a sitting position and let your eyes adjust to the dark. After a few seconds, you notice an opening farther down the tunnel.

You look more closely. The opening looks more like a real doorway than another cave tunnel. And wait—is that a torch in a bracket beside it? Maybe your luck is changing.

GO ON TO THE NEXT PAGE.

HOW DO I GET THIS TO--

--LIGHT!

NOWHERE TO GO BUT FORWARD.

YOU WALK FOR WHAT SEEMS TO BE AN HOUR WITH NOTHING BUT THE TORCH, THE WALLS, AND YOURSELF. IT MAKES YOU NERVOUS.

THE FARTHER YOU GO, THE HARDER IT WILL BE TO DEFEND YOURSELF IF YOU ARE ATTACKED.

NO ROOM TO MOVE.

THIS CAN'T BE GOOD.

NO, IT'S NOT GOOD, BUT IS THAT WHAT YOU THINK IT IS?

IT IS! IT'S A SWORD... STUCK IN A PIECE OF STONE.

GO ON TO THE NEXT PAGE.

You pull the sword. It's light, easy to swing. The shield is just as light and decorated with a single white stripe down the middle.

WILL YOU

carry your discoveries...

...to the left?

TURN TO PAGE 66.

...to the right?

TURN TO PAGE 111.

You look up into the golden eyes of the dragon Gartrugh. "When I started out, I just wanted to be a famous hero."

"Is that what you still want?" Gartrugh bends his neck and comes closer to you.

"I think so." You stop for a second and purse your lips. "But I don't know where to start."

Gartrugh gestures with his wings toward the treasure in the rooms. "Why, here. You will be the hero of Mount Fate. You will right wrongs and help those in need. My sons will help you." Gartrugh points at himself with one claw. "I will help you learn magic and other skills."

You turn to look at Wizard Uchawi and the Lady of the Mount. "What about them?"

"The wizard will be allowed to do what he wishes. The Lady will stay because she is doing what she does. But what will *you* do?"

GO ON TO THE NEXT PAGE.

The tunnel is damp but dry. Your fingertips touch the rough surface of the carved stone walls. They look like bricks. But somebody—probably somebodies—carved the stone to make it look so.

A faint tickle of breeze pushes you from behind, urging you on. The air smells faintly dusty, like a storeroom. Maybe you should turn around and go back and . . .

Wait. A glint of light catches your eye. Something shiny, but not another light. Maybe a reflection? There must be something up ahead, something valuable.

TURN TO PAGE 91.

The torches go out, but Wizard Uchawi's magic wand sprouts a light. "You lead the way," he says.

You walk for what seems forever, turning left and right in the twisting hall. The walls change from smooth to bricked to rough, then back to smooth again. It's strangely silent. The only sounds you hear are your breathing and the *clunkety-clunk* of Wizard Uchawi's possessions bouncing about.

"I think we're going in circles," you say as you lean against a wall to catch your breath.

"I don't think so," says the wizard. He points ahead with his wand.

*"Libbety, lobbity, led,
Light, show us what's ahead."*

The globe grows bigger, then shoots a beam of light. Fifty feet away, a lady dressed in a pink gown glitters.

"Hmmm, the Lady of the Mount." Wizard Uchawi smiles. "I think we should talk to her, don't you?"

You nod, not knowing what else to say.

60   GO ON TO THE NEXT PAGE.

The Lady smiles as you approach. Wizard Uchawi kneels and nudges you to do so as well.

"Adventurers, to save the mountain, I offer you a choice and a reward. You may face the dragon, you may face the genie, or you may face the ooze."

WILL YOU CHOOSE...

...the dragon?
TURN TO PAGE 31.

...the ooze?
TURN TO PAGE 45.

...the genie?
TURN TO PAGE 82.

SHOOOSH

WHOA!

SLAMM!

WHAT'S THIS?

REST FOR A BIT.

WHO'S THERE!

SHOW YOURSELF!

SILLY, SILLY HERO. RELAX, DRINK, AND MAKE READY.

I CAN NEITHER HARM YOU NOR HELP YOU. I CAN JUST MAKE LIFE A LITTLE EASIER FOR NOW.

The voice is a bit gurgly. "I am a water sprite, hero, and I help those who enter this little room. High King Elodorat had it carved hundreds of years ago, when he fought the dragons. It's been years since anyone visited. Are you a soldier of the new High King?"

"No," you answer. "I'm on an adventure. I just escaped the borkadrac."

"A borkadrac? My, those are nasty creatures. Never bathe. Did you know that? It's gone now, though. I can tell. Have a drink," the sprite continues. "It will help."

You relax and take a gulp. The water is so cold, your head aches. But the sprite is right—it feels good.

"Can I take any of these?" you ask as you point at the arms.

"You can, but only one."

You take a shield. It would have been helpful against the borkadrac.

GO ON TO THE NEXT PAGE.

As the sprite speaks, you notice a tunnel leading out of the room. A magic torch lights the way.

WILL YOU...

...leave the room and head down the mountain?

TURN TO PAGE 78.

...go into the tunnel?

TURN TO PAGE 59.

You have the lamp in your hands, but you don't know what to do with it. You've heard stories of rubbing a genie's lamp to command him, but they were just that—stories. The wizard will know what to do.

You reach back and throw the lamp toward Wizard Uchawi.

It arcs through the air, its polished surface glinting in the cavern's light. As the lamp leaves your hands, the genie bursts free!

"Nooo!" yells Wizard Uchawi.

"Yes!" booms the genie.

The room crackles with energy, and you shut your eyes.

The air goes warm, and it grows hard to breathe. You reach out and touch glass. When you open your eyes, you see you're in a small glass room. You pound on the glass, but it's unbreakable. You look left, right, up, and down. All around you are others just like you. People who thought they would be heroes.

Instead, they are stuck here, collected like dolls in the genie's cavern.

THE END

You turn to the left, gripping the sword. You couldn't hide your grin even if you tried. Your only regret is that you have no one to show this sword to. It feels like a part of you, swinging easily, not the slightest balance problem or awkwardness. Maybe it's magic.

The hall is remarkably silent. You can hear your own heartbeat as you walk forward. Your footsteps echo away. Even the sound of your sword's scabbard slapping against you is loud. If any enemies are about down here, they'll hear you coming long before you know they're around.

That is not a comforting thought.

TWISTED JOURNEYS™

"Well? Are you going to help me or not? If so, I have more packing to do and if not, then I'd rather stop packing, if you don't mind," says the wizard as he looks over his spectacles at you.

WILL YOU...

...stall for time by saying you don't know if you can help?

TURN TO PAGE 16.

...say no?

TURN TO PAGE 28.

...say yes?

TURN TO PAGE 102.

At first you slide slowly down the slimy tunnel, but you build up speed. Zooming from side to side, you become covered in slime. Your sword tumbles free, as does the torch.

Suddenly, you feel nothing beneath you. Then you hit hard ground. You tumble head over heels, finally stopping in a pile of muck, sharp sticks, and stones.

You shake your head. Your eyes adjust to the darkness. Your torch lies a good distance away, still flaming, lighting the wall. Something is written there—and there's someone sitting there, too!

"Hello!" you yell as you make your way toward the torch.

Then you see. The someone isn't anyone, at least not anyone alive. It's a skeleton.

You realize the sticks on the ground aren't sticks, but bones. The room is full of skeletons.

The writing on the wall? "NO ESCAPE" is all it says. And it's right.

THE END

The thunderous roar of the fireball makes your ears ring. You pull the shield up over your head and hope it will be enough.

Too late, you realize this was the wrong choice.

The fireball burns thoroughly, so hot that it leaves nothing in its wake. The hall goes dark and silent. No one will ever know you were here.

THE END

It's right there behind you. The borkadrac's hot, steamy breath makes you want to throw up. You twist aside, pulling at the branches of the bushes around you.

You want to scream, but there's no time. You force your way through the bushes, letting the branches go. They flap by you, slapping the monster. Maybe they'll hurt it enough to help you get away.

You don't know where you're going. You just run. You push brush out of the way, snap branches, and stomp on dead twigs. You're too noisy. You don't have a chance of the borkadrac not catching you. Your only hope is to keep running. Running fast. Running far.

72

GO ON TO THE NEXT PAGE.

Before you is a stony trail that leads up the mountain. To the right is a narrow trail, probably used by mountain goats, that leads down.

Hurry, hurry, if you take too long you're going to be borkadrac feed!

WILL YOU...

...head down the mountain?

TURN TO PAGE 22.

...head up the mountain?

TURN TO PAGE 98.

You scamper backward, your head swiveling between the door and the soldiers. They keep clumping toward you, their heavy steps echoing in the hallway. Their pounding weight makes vibrations so strong that you feel like the whole hallway could cave in.

You reach for the door handle, but first you check the soldiers again. You've got enough time to look away...for a moment.

You pull on the handle, but the door doesn't budge.

You push on the handle, but the door still doesn't budge.

Locked! You groan.

GO ON TO THE NEXT PAGE.

Of all the rotten luck. There's no time to think. You turn to face the soldiers.

Wait. The sword is magic. It cuts through stone...What else does it cut through?

WILL YOU...

...stand and fight the soldiers with your magic sword and shield?

TURN TO PAGE 33.

...strike the door with your magic sword?

TURN TO PAGE 87.

You jump up and snag the rope. You get both hands on it and wrap it around each wrist. It feels a bit tight, but looking down, you realize you have no option but to hold on or to fall hundreds of feet onto the rocks below.

Wizard Uchawi turns and smiles. "I thought you were pretty smart." He gestures with his hand, and the rope softens, but it still holds you securely. "I'll be needing a servant in River City, and I think you'll prove to be the one."

A servant! No! You were going to be a hero. That's why Alaric taught you all those fighting skills.

You can't let go of the rope— it's holding you snugly. You doubt it'll let go when you land, either.

Servant? Not likely. You're going to be a slave.

THE END

GO ON TO THE NEXT PAGE.

A simple life with no adventure is not a bad life. You will marry, have children, and enjoy every day. You will rescue a starving dog, which you'll name Bounder. He'll go everywhere you go.

You'll also have the tale of how you fought a borkadrac, met a water sprite, and found a shield. And later, when you're much older, your grandchildren will ask to hear it over and over again, to your delight.

THE END

You take the fight to the beast. If you're meant to be a hero, you'll earn it here on the side of Mount Fate. You swing your sword just as you were trained to do.

This beast will be your claim to fame. From its hide you will make boots that are like no others. People will speak your name in awe as they sing the song of your deeds.

But the beast steps backward. It keeps itself just out of reach of your sword.

GO ON TO THE NEXT PAGE.

81

The Lady of the Mount touches your head. Everything goes blue.

You open your eyes to a sparkling pile of gold, sapphires, rubies, diamonds, shields, urns, and much more. You mouth the word "wow," but no sound comes out.

"My, my. I am impressed." Wizard Uchawi holds up a ruby the size of his palm.

"I do not think I am." The voice thunders through the room, shaking the air and causing a pile of coins to avalanche.

You look up and see above you a man at least fifty feet tall with long hair and a full beard. He wears a turban with a giant diamond clasp and gold rings on every finger.

You point at him with your sword. "You must be the genie."

The genie laughs and gestures to glass cages with heroes like you locked within. "And you must be next."

GO ON TO THE NEXT PAGE.

GO ON TO THE NEXT PAGE.

83

TWISTED JOURNEYS™

You have the lamp. The genie is
trapped. Now what?

WILL YOU...

...rub the lamp, hoping the genie will
come out and do your bidding?
TURN TO PAGE 35.

...throw the lamp to
Wizard Uchawi?
TURN TO PAGE 65.

No, you tell yourself, others have been here already. They would have taken whatever treasure was here. You reach up to place the torch back into the bracket. A giggle stops you. It sounds like fingernails scraping across a child's writing slate.

"Who's there?" you ask. More giggles. You feel goosebumps form all over your body. That giggle isn't a giggle at all. It's the sound of goblins talking.

With a *snickety-shoosh*, you pull your sword. You grab your shield with your other hand. It only sounds like four or five. Nothing you can't handle.

GO ON TO THE NEXT PAGE.

You were wrong. There are quite a few more than four or five.

About ten times that many.

They close in on you, pressing hard. You try to swing your sword, but you can't because they're grabbing your arm. They even grab at your shield.

Before you know it, you're being dragged away along the tunnel. The goblins pull you down a passage you hadn't noticed, one where the breeze is quite strong. You realize you should have thought more about that tickling breeze you'd felt behind you. Too late now, though. You're going to spend the rest of your life as a goblin slave, carving tunnels in the mountains as your captors mine for their precious goblin rocks.

THE END

87

You press the down arrow, and the doors open to show a small, boxlike room.

"This doesn't seem quite right," says Wizard Uchawi. "I wish my magic wand was working."

You both step inside. The doors whoosh shut. Your legs go light, and you feel like you're moving downward. Then the movement stops.

The door opens, and a big beast covered with hair grabs you and hands you a pickaxe. Another one, just like him, does the same with Wizard Uchawi.

The beasts push you down a walkway and into a dark cave spotted with little torches. You see creatures of all types swinging pickaxes at the walls, pushing carts, or carrying rocks.

The beast pushes you forward. "GET TO WORK, SLAVE!"

"How do we get out of here?" you whisper to Wizard Uchawi, but he just waves his broken wand .

"I don't think we do. I think we're here forever," he says as a beast drags him away.

THE END

Your feet slide a bit as you stand to fight, but the slick ground works in your favor, too. A soldier swings at you and misses. The force of his swing takes him too far, and he slips on the slime. He slides down the tunnel, flailing silently.

You turn back—too slowly. The butt of an axe strikes your shoulder. It hurts. It burns.

You lift your hand. Your fingers won't bend! As you look at it, the soldiers stop attacking. Your hand is all smooth and waxy looking. Before your very eyes, it begins to drip.

You look down at your feet, but they're not there! They've melted away in a slimy mess.

Oh no. This hallway must be cursed. Any living thing—like you—turns to slime.

Time seems to come to a stop as you slowly melt. Your clothes and armor fall away, and at last you are absorbed into the slime that is all that remains of those who came before you.

THE END

You take down a torch from the wall and poke it into the hole. Cobwebs grab at you, but you brush them away. A tiny black beetle skitters into the darkness.

WILL YOU...

...go into the new tunnel?
TURN TO PAGE 50.

...turn around and go back?
TURN TO PAGE 85.

You turn and charge the army of little spiders. You stamp and you stomp and you slap and you swing, hitting spiders with every movement.

But for every ten you take down, at least ten more seem to fill their places. They're everywhere. Crawling on you arms, on your legs, across your chest, in your hair. And they bite.

You keep moving, but the bites start to sting. The spiders are inside your clothes, down your back, inside your boots.

You throw yourself against the walls, hoping to crush some. Your eyesight gets blurry. Your legs feel heavy, each step slower and slower, until you tumble down.

The spiders keep crawling over you, but you can't feel them anymore. There's no more pain as they begin to wrap you up in their silky webs, preparing to store you for a later feast for their colony.

THE END

94

TURN TO PAGE 8.

You look down and then back at the rope. If you jump and miss, you'll plunge hundreds of feet to your death on the rocks below.

You go back to the staircase. You step onto the steps, but they're still turning upward. You can't run down fast enough to make any progress. In fact, the staircase keeps throwing you off, like a small spinning catapult.

Next you look for a down arrow like the one you saw inside, but there's nothing. Just you and the turning stairs to keep you company.

You look around and realize you can see for miles, and in all of those miles there's nobody to see you. You made it to the top of Mount Fate, but you have no treasure and no one even knows you got this far. Even worse, you will be stuck here at the top of the mountain... forever.

THE END

You parry attacks, occasionally striking one of the stone soldiers, but you can't keep this up forever. They don't seem to tire.

You, however, have been going nonstop since you woke up this morning. You're hungry, tired, and thirsty. You need a break, but you won't be getting one soon. The soldiers just keep on coming at you. Every sculpture you pass becomes another soldier. One replaces every one you defeat.

If you stop, you don't know what will happen to you, but if you continue, you can't be sure either.

As you shuffle backward down the tunnel, you realize that the air is getting a bit cooler and a bit damper. The walls seem almost greasy from some sort of slime growing on them.

Your foot slides out from under you and you fall, sliding backward.

GO ON TO THE NEXT PAGE.

TWISTED JOURNEYS™

You look up from the hard floor. The stone soldiers are still walking toward you, with more and more appearing behind them.

WILL YOU...

...pull yourself up to fight?
TURN TO PAGE 69.

...let yourself slide down the tunnel, knowing you can't beat the soldiers?
TURN TO PAGE 90.

GO ON TO THE NEXT PAGE.

Your knees knock. What to do, what to do? Before you had someplace to turn, someplace to run, but coming up the mountain was a bad choice. You have no escape.

Your stomach gurgles, and it feels like a thousand butterflies are flitting about inside. Your mouth dries. Your teeth stick to the inside of your mouth. You run your tongue over them, wetting them with what little spittle you have.

Under your feet, loose stones skritch about as you slide a step backward, hoping to get a bit of balance. The beast watches you, its glistening eyes tracking your every movement. It almost seems to be waiting for you to slip before it strikes.

You reach out, and your hand brushes something smooth. You turn to see a small shield carved into the rock. The shield gives a bit when you press it.

The borkadrac roars and draws your attention. It's now or never. You spring forward, pushing off your back foot. You land on your front foot and regain your balance. It's a risky move, and Alaric would never commend you for it. Sloppy footwork, he would call it.

You push forward with your sword arm, hoping to strike a point where the borkadrac is weak. You hear the delightful sound of the monster roaring.

The beast twists in pain, pulling your sword with it. You tug back, pulling the sword free, and step backward. Your ankle still hurts. You brace yourself against the mountain wall, keeping your sword ready.

You reach for the wall for balance and press the stone shield again. You know you're close to defeating this beast.

GO ON TO THE NEXT PAGE.

The borkadrac lowers its head and bounds toward you. Small rocks skitter from the force of its claws as it closes in.

WILL YOU...

...press the shield?
TURN TO PAGE 62.

...strike with your sword to defend yourself?
TURN TO PAGE 80.

102

TURN TO PAGE 40.

You run back and grab Wizard Uchawi and pull him along with you. But the entrances to the room have disappeared. The walls show no trace that two doorways ever existed.

You look down at your boots and slump your shoulders. "How long?"

Wizard Uchawi looks at you. He waits before he answers. "Until the next hero comes along."

"How long will that be?" You sit on a very large pillow. It's soft, and the velvet covering tickles your fingers.

"I waited over nine hundred years for you. It could easily be that long again."

"Nine hundred years! I'll be dead."

"No, not in here. You won't age a day." Wizard Uchawi smiles. "Do you play chess?"

"No, I don't know how."

"Well, then, I'll teach you. You have all the time in the world to learn."

THE END

You scramble hand over hand to the back of the hall. The glow of the fireball is immense and seems even hotter than before. Your skin stings from the heat, and you have to squint to protect your eyes.

You pull yourself up to your feet and see a metal bar attached to a chain that runs to a pulley in the wall. The heat is getting worse. You know you won't make it if you stay here.

You stand up. The handle is just out of reach. So close...

The heat grows, and you swear you can smell your hair as it singes.

You jump for the bar. Your fingers close around the cool metal, and you let gravity take over.

The chain groans a bit but gives just as the heat becomes unbearable.

Below, the floor grinds and opens. A trapdoor!

Wizard Uchawi arches an eyebrow. "You're braver than I thought."

It's time to tighten the belt and head forward. You look at Uchawi. "Where does this go?"

The wizard rolls his eyes and throws his hands up. "How should I know? I've been cooped up in a room for nine hundred years."

Fine, you tell yourself. Obviously this hidden hallway must be important, or it wouldn't be hidden, right? "We go this way." You take out your sword and grip your shield.

Wizard Uchawi softly harrumphs, "This got me in trouble last time," but he follows.

GO ON TO THE NEXT PAGE.

GO ON TO THE NEXT PAGE.

No compass. Two doors. Three choices.

WILL YOU...

…press the up arrow?
TURN TO PAGE 48.

…press the down arrow?
TURN TO PAGE 88.

…open the glowing door?
TURN TO PAGE 110.

You lunge at the big spider, stabbing, swinging, even clubbing with your shield, but the shiny hairs all over its body protect it. You can't get a clean shot.

A mighty lunge sends your sword beyond the spider's hairy armor and wriggling limbs. Gooey green gel drips out as you withdraw the sword. The spider jumps, and you move in to strike another blow. Something wet drips on your arm. It stings and burns a bit.

You swing your sword, but the spider dips out of the way, and you feel a fang strike you on the back. The wound hurts for only a second. Then you can't feel your fingers—or anything else for that matter.

In moments, you are wrapped in spider silk. The spider drags you back to its lair, where it will store you for a later day.

THE END

The glowing door leads to another one, which is covered with markings you don't understand and gems you've never seen. This has to be it. This has to be the treasure trove.

"I don't think that's where we want to go," Wizard Uchawi says. He stands back and shakes his head. "It looks awfully familiar."

You open the door. Beyond you see gold coins piled high. Treasure chests overflow with pearl necklaces, gems, and more. You want to say something, but words escape you.

"Don't go in there," Wizard Uchawi says behind you.

You step into the room.

"It's just like—"

The door slams shut, cutting off Wizard Uchawi's words. The lights go dark, then flash back on.

The room is empty except for a couch, a fountain, and a table. You spin around. It looks just like the place where you found Wizard Uchawi.

The place where *you'll* be trapped for at least nine hundred years, too.

THE END

TURN TO PAGE 38.

READY FOR MORE ADVENTURES?

WHICH **TWISTED JOURNEYS**

WILL YOU TRY NEXT?

#1 CAPTURED BY PIRATES
Danger on the high seas! A band of scurvy pirates has boarded your ship. Can you keep them from turning you into shark bait?

#2 ESCAPE FROM PYRAMID X
You're on an archaeological mission to an ancient pyramid, complete with ancient mummies. Unfortunately for you, not everything that's ancient is also dead...

#3 TERROR IN GHOST MANSION
Halloween's not supposed to be this scary. You and your friends are trapped in a creepy old house with a bunch of spooks. And they definitely aren't wearing costumes...

#4 THE TREASURE OF MOUNT FATE
Plenty of people have braved the monsters and magic of Mount Fate in search of its legendary treasure. But no one has ever lived to brag about their quest. Will you be the first?